One Nosy PUP

by Carol Wallace

illustrated by Steve Björkman

SCHOLASTIC INC.

New York Toronto London Auckland Sydney
Mexico City New Delhi Hong Kong Buenos Aires

To Diane Foote and Barbara Walsh
C. W.

For Ashley Whitt with lots of love
S. B.

ISBN 0-439-83990-4

Text copyright © 2005 by Carol Wallace.
Illustrations copyright © 2005 by Steve Björkman. All rights reserved.
Published by Scholastic Inc., 557 Broadway, New York, NY 10012,
by arrangement with Holiday House, Inc.
SCHOLASTIC and associated logos are trademarks and/or
registered trademarks of Scholastic Inc.

12 11 10 9 8 7 6 5 4 3   6 7 8 9 10/0

Printed in the U.S.A.   23

First Scholastic printing, December 2005

Contents

1. Crunch! Crunch!

Poky stretched and yawned.
He had been all over
his new house.
Now his stomach growled.
"Time for a snack," he said.
Poky walked to his bowl.
"Hey, where is my food?"

He sniffed and sniffed and sniffed.
He found one chunk of food
by the door.

Two pieces were near the fireplace.
Three were under the stove.
"Mama will think
I made this mess.
Somebody is eating my food.
I have to get the thief."

He had a plan.

He waited until night.

"Bedtime, Poky," Mama finally called.

Poky hopped up onto the bed.

He curled around Mama's feet.

He closed his eyes.

Mama and Daddy were sound asleep.

"ZZZZ. Zzzz," snored Daddy.

"ZZZZ. Zzzz," snored Mama.

Slowly, Poky slid off the bed.

Poky walked softly to his bowl.

"*Grrr*," Poky growled.

"That thief has been here."

Poky sniffed and sniffed.

Carefully, he went
into the living room.
Crunch. Crunch. Crunch.
The noise came
from the fireplace.
Sniff. Sniff. Sniff.
Poky's nose wiggled.
Crunch. Crunch. Crunch.

Poky crept closer.
Sniff. Sniff. Sniff.
"What's all the sniffing?"
a little voice asked.
"You are one nosy pup."

Poky jumped back.

"Who said that?"

There was no answer.

Poky plopped down.

He sat there all night.

He listened.

It was quiet all night long.

"I'll try again tomorrow."

The next night Poky slipped
off the bed.
At the end of the hall
he stopped.
He didn't hear a sound.
Suddenly, something
streaked
across the floor.

Poky watched it scamper
around the room.
He peered behind the couch.
He listened.
Crunch. Crunch.

"Hey, you!

What are you doing?"

Poky yipped quietly.

Small brown eyes peered back.

"I'm having a little snack."

The animal sat on his back legs.

Poky stared at the brown thing.

"That is *my* snack!

Who are you anyway?

Why are you eating my food?

Where did you come from?"

2. Charlie

Poky squinted at the creature.

"The name is Charlie.

I am Charlie the hamster."

Charlie stared at Poky.

"Why are you eating my food?"

Poky asked.

"No one was eating it,"

Charlie answered.

"Free food!"

Charlie crunched and crunched.
"Where did you come from?"
Poky asked.
"I've lived here a long time,"
said the hamster.

"My boy, Adam,

used to take care of me.

Sometimes I left my cage.

I would explore.

Then I'd go back.

But one day my cage was gone.

My boy was gone.

Everybody was gone.

Then you and your family came.

Free food!" Charlie said.

"You do not have to steal food,"
Poky said.
"My nice family will feed you."

"Do you have a boy?" Charlie asked.

"No. Just Mama and Daddy. Why?"

Charlie rubbed his whiskers.

"Boys like hamsters.

Most grown-ups do not."

Poky wagged his tail.

"You'll like my family."

Charlie frowned. "Thank you.
But I think I'd better stay away.
I have to go now."
Charlie wiggled into a crack
beside the fireplace.
"By the way, what's your name?"
The voice came from the fireplace.
"I'm Poky. Poky the beagle."
"We'll talk again," the voice called.
From then on Poky always left food
for Charlie.
Charlie always
cleaned up.
Things were
going well, until . . .

"Come on, Poky," Mama called.
"You're going to Amy's.
The kids can't wait to see you.
We have to go out of town.
We'll be back on Monday."
Poky had a great weekend.
Amy and Kit and the kids
kept him busy.

He forgot all about Charlie.

Until he came in the door . . .

"What in the world?" Mama gasped.

"There must be a mouse," Daddy said.

"No, I think it was a rat!"
Mama said.

All the kitchen cabinet
doors were open.

Boxes were on the floor.

Cereal was everywhere.

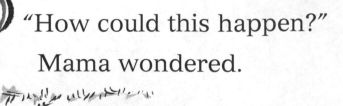

"How could this happen?"
Mama wondered.

Poky knew.

He walked over to the fireplace.

"Charlie!" Poky whispered.

"Hey, Mama,
I think Poky's found something."

Daddy dropped down onto his knees.

He looked into the fireplace.

"I'll get the traps," Daddy said.

3. Snap!

That night Poky walked quietly
into the living room.
"Traps!" Poky yipped.
"I know. I saw them,"
Charlie called.
"They hid your bowl.
The only food is in the traps."

Charlie squeezed out
of his hiding place.
"I can trip the traps," said Poky.
Poky walked to his toy box.
He pulled out his ball.

Poky dropped the ball.
SNAP! went the trap.

Poky rolled the ball
at the second one.
SNAP! went
the second trap.

"I think there is one more,"
Charlie said.

Poky sniffed and sniffed.
"HERE it is. I'll get it!"
Poky rolled the ball at the trap.
SNAP! went the last one.
"Thanks, Poky."

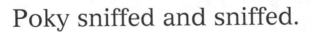

Charlie munched.

Poky crept back to bed.

He curled around Mama's feet.

"Hey!" Mama yelled the next morning.

Daddy ran into the room.

"The traps are empty," Mama said.

"I know what to do," Daddy said.

Daddy started crashing around
in the closet.

"Here it is," he said.

"We'll get to the bottom of this."

4. Solving the Puzzle

That night the lights
in the living room were still on.
"Charlie? Are you there, Charlie?"
Poky sniffed at the fireplace.
"I'm in here," Charlie said.
"The lights are still on."
Poky looked all around the room.
"They forgot to turn them off."

Charlie rubbed his tummy.

"Can you trip those traps again?

I'm hungry!"

Poky got his ball.

He started to work.

Charlie nibbled at the food.

"Thanks. You are a super pal,"

Charlie said.

Poky and Charlie talked for hours.

Finally, Poky slipped back

into the bedroom.

When Poky woke up,
Mama was in the living room.
"Look at them." She laughed.
Daddy pointed to
the television screen.

"They seem to know each other.

I know what to do.

Come on," Daddy said.

They went out the door.

Daddy had a huge trap.

Poky was scared.

He had to warn Charlie.

He couldn't find him anywhere.

I'll tell him tonight, Poky thought.

That night Daddy set up the trap.
Then he made Poky come to bed.
Poky waited.
"ZZZZ. Zzzz," snored Daddy.
"ZZZZ. Zzzz," snored Mama.
Poky slid off the bed.
He shoved his nose
against the door.
Nothing happened.
He bumped his head
against the wood.
Mama and Daddy
had shut the door!

Poky hopped back onto the bed.

He worried all night long.

Charlie was in trouble.

Mama opened the door

in the morning.

Poky ran to warn Charlie.

He was too late!

Charlie was in the trap.

"Did the trap hurt you?"

Poky asked.

"I'll try to get you out."

Charlie smiled.
"I don't want to get out.
This is not a trap.
This is a hamster house.
I have an exercise wheel.
I even have hamster food.
I'm tired of dog food."

Charlie loved his new house.

Poky came to visit.

Sometimes Poky let Charlie out.

They shared Poky's dog food.

They ran and played.

At bedtime Poky curled
around Mama's feet.

But first he always made sure that
Charlie was safe.